This *LADYBIRD TALE*
belongs to

....

Hansel
and
Gretel

Retold by Vera Southgate M.A., B.COM
with illustrations by Adrienne Salgado

LADYBIRD 🐞 TALES

ONCE UPON A TIME there were two children, a boy called Hansel and a girl called Gretel. They lived with their father and stepmother in a little cottage at the edge of a forest.

Their father was a woodcutter, and he was very poor. One day, he had so little money that he could no longer give his family enough to eat. This made him very unhappy.

"How can we feed the children?" he asked his wife one night. "We have just enough for two, but not for four."

His wife did not really like the children. "I know what we must do," she replied. "Tomorrow we will take the children into the thickest part of the forest. Then we must leave them there. They will never find their way home. We shall be free of them!"

"I could never do that," said the woodcutter. "How can you even think of such a thing?"

"You fool!" his wife cried. "Then all four of us will die of hunger!"

The woodcutter's wife gave him no peace, until at last he agreed.

Too hungry to sleep, Hansel and
Gretel overheard what was said.
Gretel cried bitterly.

"Don't worry," said Hansel.
"I will look after you."

Once his parents were asleep,
he crept quietly outside. White
pebbles lay around, like silver
coins in the moonlight. He filled
his pockets with them, and went
back to bed.

Early next morning, the
woodcutter's wife wakened the
two children. "We are going into
the forest to chop wood," she
told them.

As they walked along, Hansel kept glancing back at the cottage. "Hansel, why are you lagging behind?" asked his father.

"My white cat is on the roof, Father," said Hansel. "I am trying to say goodbye."

"It's the sun shining on the white chimney, you silly boy," said his stepmother.

But Hansel wasn't really looking at a cat. Each time he stopped, he dropped a pebble from his pocket onto the path.

When they came to the middle of the forest, the woodcutter said, "I will make a fire so you won't be cold."

"We are going to chop wood," their stepmother said. "We will come for you when we are ready."

Hansel and Gretel sat by the fire. Then they waited for their parents to come. They waited so long that they fell asleep.

When they woke, it was dark. Gretel was frightened.

"Wait until the moon comes up," Hansel comforted her. "Then we will find our way home."

At last the moon rose in the sky. Hansel took his sister's hand, and followed the pebbles he had left on the path. They shone like silver coins in the moonlight and showed the children the way home.

"You naughty children!" scolded their stepmother. "Where have you been?"

The woodcutter was very happy to see them. It had broken his heart to leave them in the forest.

Before long, the family had very little food again. One night the children heard their stepmother talking to their father.

"We have half a loaf of bread left," she told him. "Once that is gone, we will have nothing. We must take the children deeper into the forest. This time they must not find their way home!"

The woodcutter's heart was heavy. He would rather have shared his last crust with his children. But his wife would not listen to his pleading, and again he had to agree.

As soon as the woodcutter and his wife were asleep, Hansel got up to fill his pockets with pebbles as before. But his stepmother had locked the door. Sadly, he went back to bed.

"Don't cry, Gretel," he said bravely. "All will be well, you'll see."

Early next morning, the stepmother wakened the children. Before they left for the forest, she gave them each a very small piece of bread.

As they walked through the trees, Hansel lagged behind and stopped every now and then.

"Hansel, why do you keep stopping?" his father asked.

"I'm looking back at my little dove," Hansel replied. "He's nodding goodbye to me."

"That isn't a dove, you foolish boy," said the stepmother. "It's the sun, shining on the chimney."
But Hansel wasn't looking at the dove. Each time he stopped, he dropped a crumb of bread on to the path.

The woodcutter's wife led the children to a part of the forest they didn't know. "Stay here," she told them. "We're going into the forest to cut wood. We'll fetch you in the evening."

At noon, Gretel shared her small piece of bread with Hansel and they lay down to wait. But when evening arrived no one came.

"Don't be afraid, Gretel," Hansel said. "When the moon comes up, we will see the crumbs of bread I dropped. They will lead us home."

Soon the moon shone, but they couldn't see any crumbs. The birds had eaten them all!

Hansel and Gretel walked all night, and all next day, and they were still deep in the forest. They were so tired they could go no further, and they lay down under a tree to sleep.

Next morning the children walked on. They were very hungry.
By midday Hansel felt they must get help soon, or they would die of hunger.

Just then a beautiful white bird perched on a nearby branch.
It sang so sweetly that they followed it as it flew through the trees. The bird led them straight to a little cottage!

"Look, Hansel!" cried Gretel.
"The cottage is made of bread and cakes, and the windows are made of sugar!"

Hansel broke off a piece of bread. Gretel took a bite from one of the cakes. Soon they were both munching happily.

Just then, the door opened and out came an old woman, walking on crutches.

Hansel and Gretel were so frightened, they dropped what they were eating. But the old woman smiled at them. "Come in, children!" she said.

She led them inside the little cottage. A meal of pancakes, milk and fruit lay ready on the table. In the back room were two little beds. After they had eaten, the children lay down, happy to be safe at last.

Hansel and Gretel did not know
that the old woman was really
a wicked old witch, who trapped
children. She couldn't see very
well, but she had a fine sense
of smell. She could smell children
coming.

The house of bread and cakes had
been built to tempt children in.

The witch gave an evil laugh.
"These two shall not escape!"
she cackled.

Early next morning, the witch
pulled Hansel from his bed, and
locked him in a cage. Although he
screamed, there was no one to
help him.

Gretel came next. "Get up, you lazy girl!" screeched the witch. "Cook something good for your brother. He will stay in the cage until he is fat enough for me to eat!"

Gretel began to cry, but the wicked witch only laughed at her tears.

Day after day passed. Gretel was soon tired out, for the witch made her clean and scrub, and cook huge meals for poor Hansel.

Every morning the witch went up to the cage. "Hold out your finger, Hansel," she would cackle. "Let me feel if you are fat enough to eat."

But Hansel would hold out a bone instead. The witch had such bad eyesight that she always thought it was his finger. She wondered why it grew no fatter.

Four weeks passed. Because of Hansel's clever trick, the witch thought he was still very thin. Soon she lost her patience.

"Fetch some water, Gretel!" she shrieked angrily. "This morning I will kill Hansel, and cook him."

The tears ran down Gretel's face. "First of all, we'll bake some bread," the old witch said with a sly look at Gretel. "I have already made the dough and heated the oven."

She pushed Gretel up to the oven
door. "Go on," said the witch. "See
if it's hot enough. Then we'll put
the bread in."

But she really planned to put
Gretel in the oven to bake. Then
she would eat the little girl as well
as Hansel.

Gretel had guessed what the wicked
witch was thinking. "I can't go in
there," she said. "I'm too big."

"You silly child," the witch said
angrily. "Look, I could even get
in myself!"

She bent down and put her head
into the oven. Gretel gave her a
hard push, and she fell right inside.

Shutting the iron door, Gretel bolted it. The witch couldn't get out.

Gretel ran to Hansel's cage. "The witch is dead!" she cried. "We're safe! Now I must get you out of that cage."

Gretel couldn't find the key, so she broke the lock with a poker from the fireplace. The door swung open. Hansel sprang out, like a bird from a cage. They hugged one another over and over again.

Now they had nothing to fear. And when they looked over the witch's house, they found caskets of pearls and precious stones.

"These are better than pebbles!"
said Hansel. He put as many into
his pockets as they would hold.
Gretel filled her apron.

They left the witch's cottage and
walked away through the trees.
It was dark in the forest, but when
they were lost the friendly birds
and animals showed them the way.

At last, Hansel and Gretel came to a part of the forest they knew.

They began to run, and at last came to their own home. Inside, they ran into their father's arms.

He had not had one happy moment since the children had been left in the forest. He was alone now, for their stepmother had died. "I'm so glad you've come home," he said.

Gretel shook out her apron, and pearls and diamonds rolled all over the floor. Hansel threw out one handful after another from his pockets.

Their troubles were over. From then on, the woodcutter and his children all lived happily ever after.

A History of
Hansel and Gretel

The story of *Hansel and Gretel* remains a popular children's tale today and recently inspired a Hollywood blockbuster, *Hansel and Gretel: The Witch Hunters*.

The story of *Hansel and Gretel* was first recorded by the Brothers Grimm in 1812. Their version came from storyteller Dortchen Wild who later became Wilhelm Grimm's wife. The Grimms continued to revise the story over the years before settling on their final version, published in 1857.

Some people think that this, and other tales of poverty and starvation, date back to the Middle Ages when people told folk stories to illustrate the hardships of daily life. The tale of *Hansel and Gretel* may also be a reference to the time of famine in 19th century Germany.

The tale's enduring popularity meant that it was made into an opera by Engelbert Humperdinck in 1893. This adaptation was so successful that the opera continues to be produced and shown today.

Collect more fantastic

LADYBIRD 🐞 TALES

9781409311072

9781409311119

9781409311102

9781409311126

The
Gingerbread
Man

9781409311096

The Three
Little Pigs

9781409311089

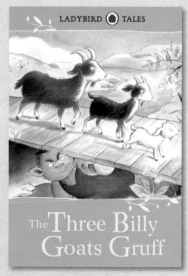

The Three Billy
Goats Gruff

9781409311065

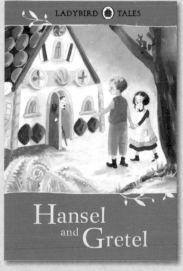

Hansel
and Gretel

9781409311133

Endpapers taken from series 606d,
first published in 1964

A catalogue record for this book is available from the British Library

Published by Ladybird Books Ltd
80 Strand London WC2R 0RL
A Penguin Company

001 – 10 9 8 7 6 5 4 3 2 1

ISBN: 978-1-40931-113-3

Printed in China